GW01339342

This book belongs to
_____

This book is dedicated
to our mom, Mary Bjelland.
We love you and miss you!

Gnome Makes Kringla

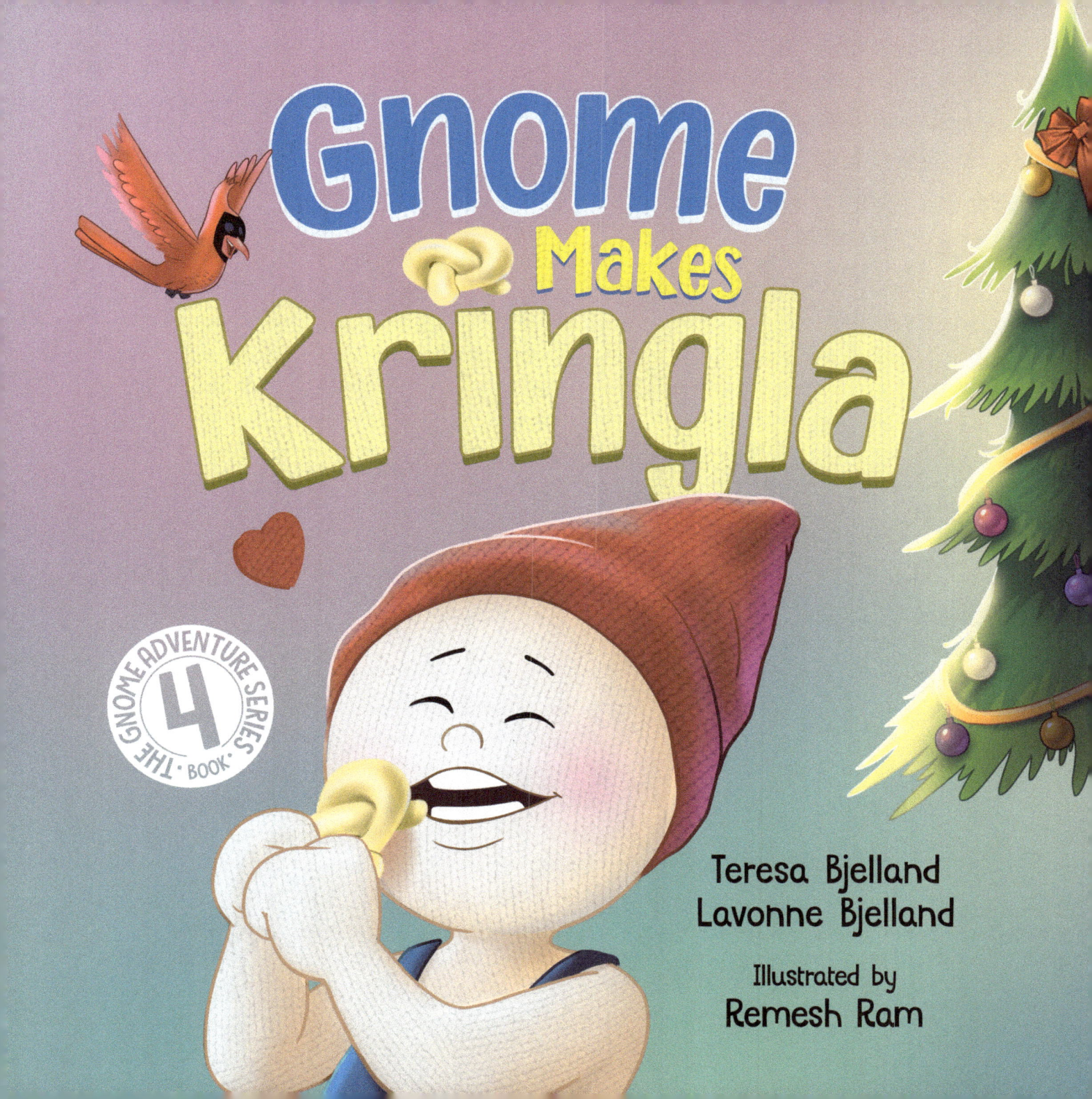

THE GNOME ADVENTURE SERIES · BOOK 4

Teresa Bjelland
Lavonne Bjelland

Illustrated by
Remesh Ram

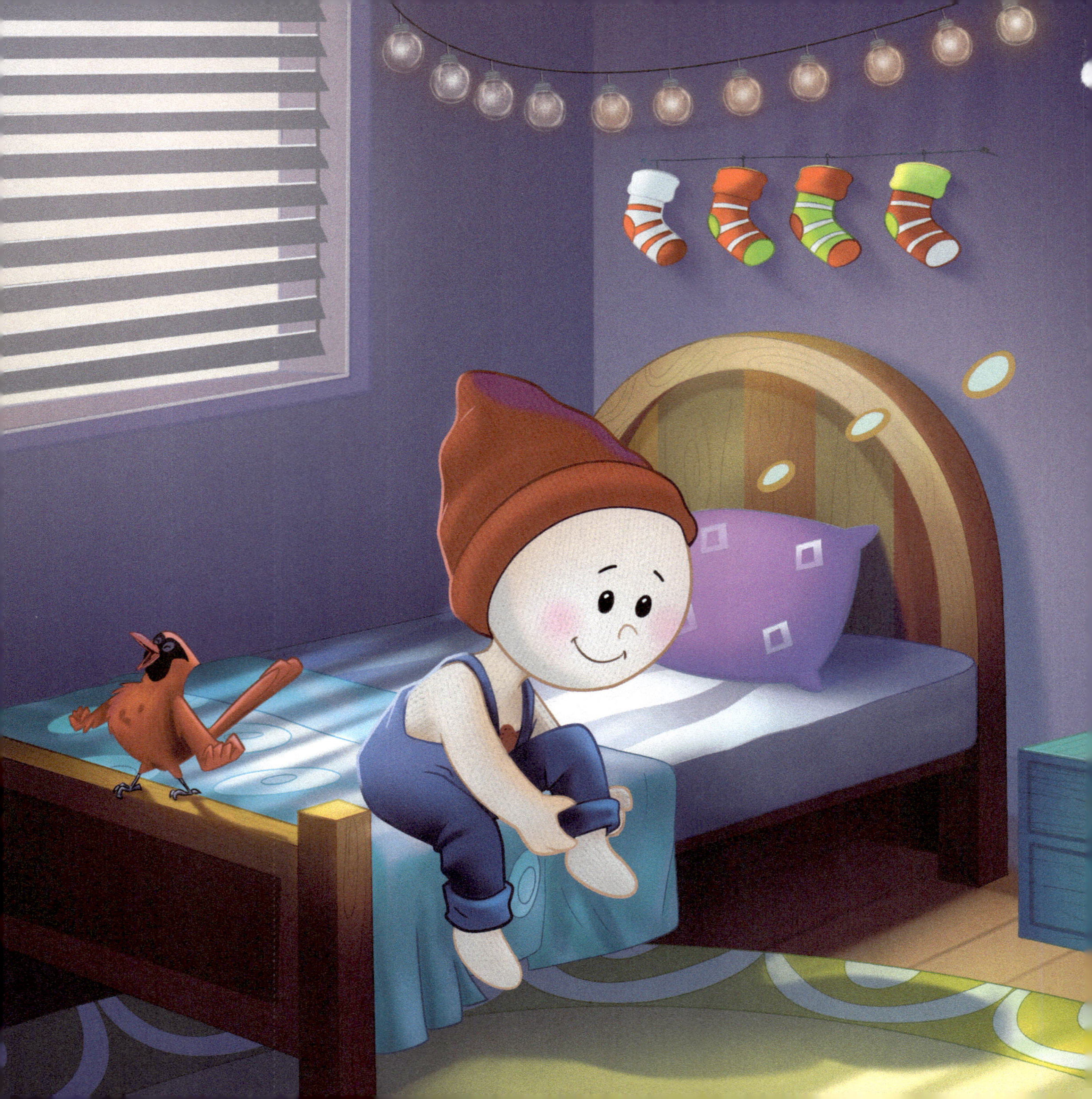

Grandma is coming to help us bake today! In Norway, Grandma's family always bakes seven different cookies for Christmas. She loves sharing cookies with friends and other family members.

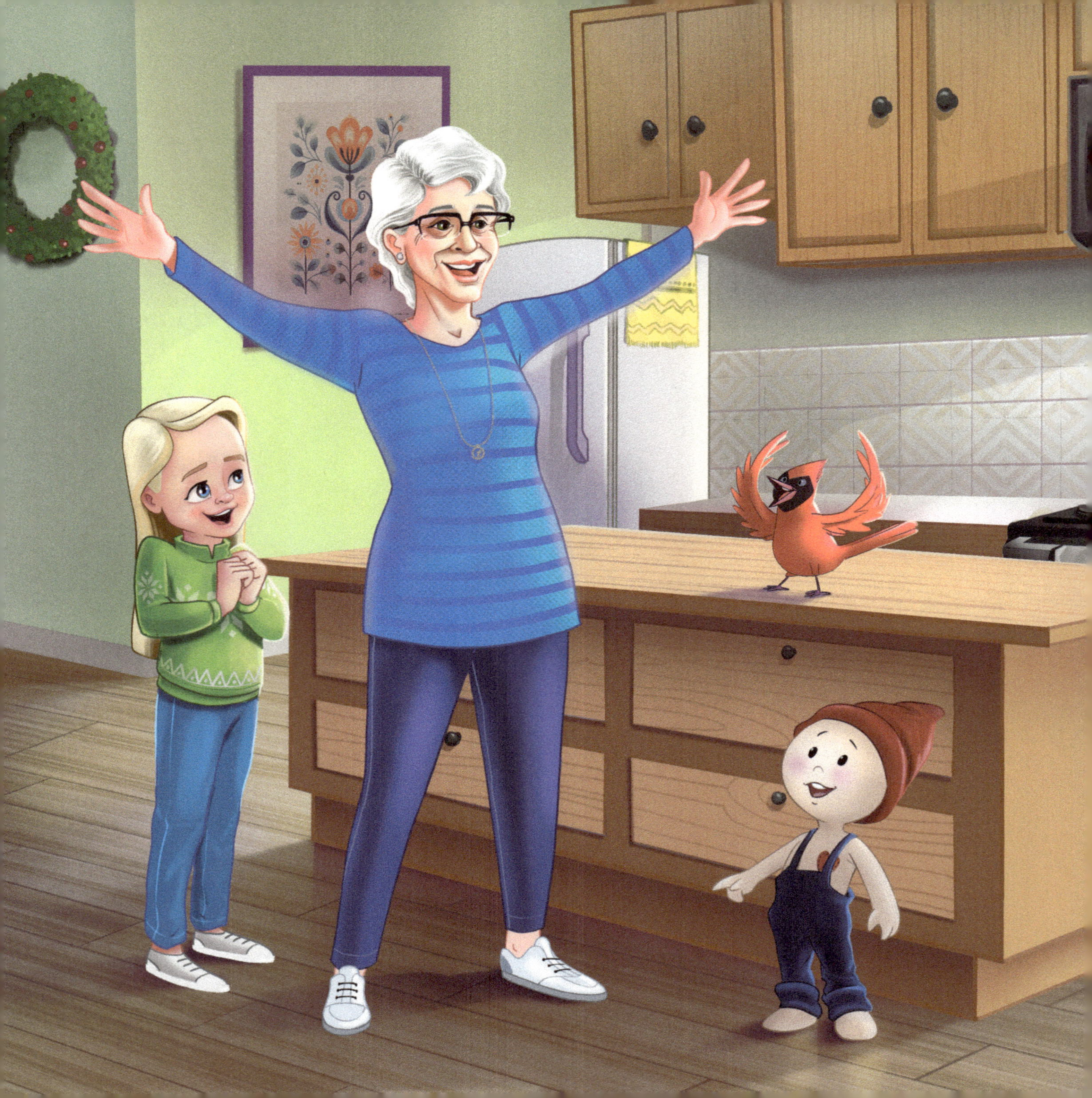

"Let's **make** Kringla!" Says Grandma. "They are soft and sweet and shaped like pretzels." "YUM!" I can't wait!

"We have a lot of work to do," Grandma says. "It takes two days and nine different ingredients to make kringla."

Kringla Recipe

1 cup granulated sugar
1/3 cup butter (softened but not melted)
1 egg
1 cup sour cream
½ cup buttermilk
½ teaspoon salt
1 teaspoon vanilla
2 teaspoons baking soda (mix in sour cream)
3 ½ cups all- purpose flour
Extra flour to roll out

We help Grandma **gather** all the ingredients.

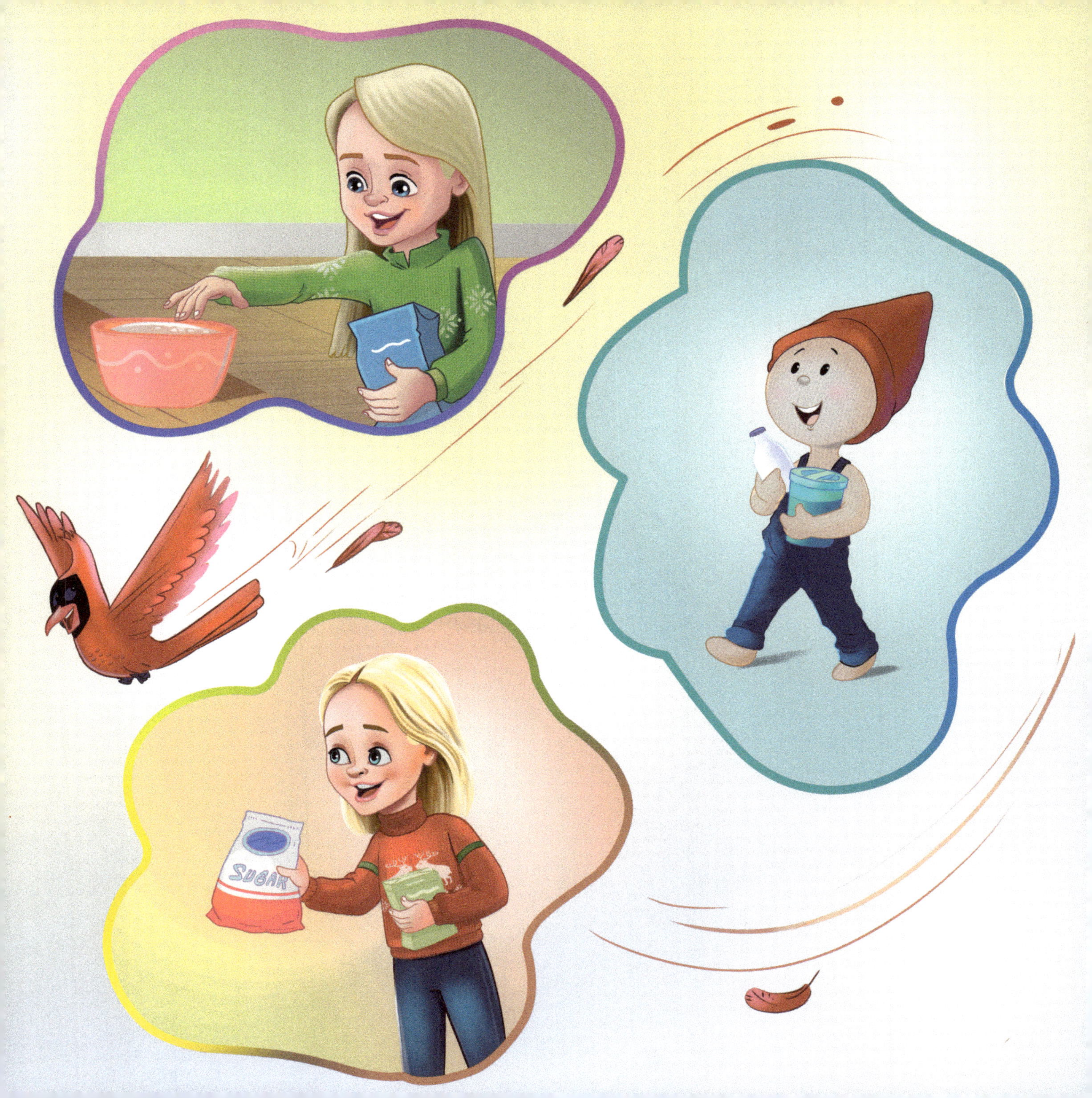
SUGAR

Oh no!
My brother dropped the **eggs.**

Oh dear!
My sister spilled the flour.

What a mess!

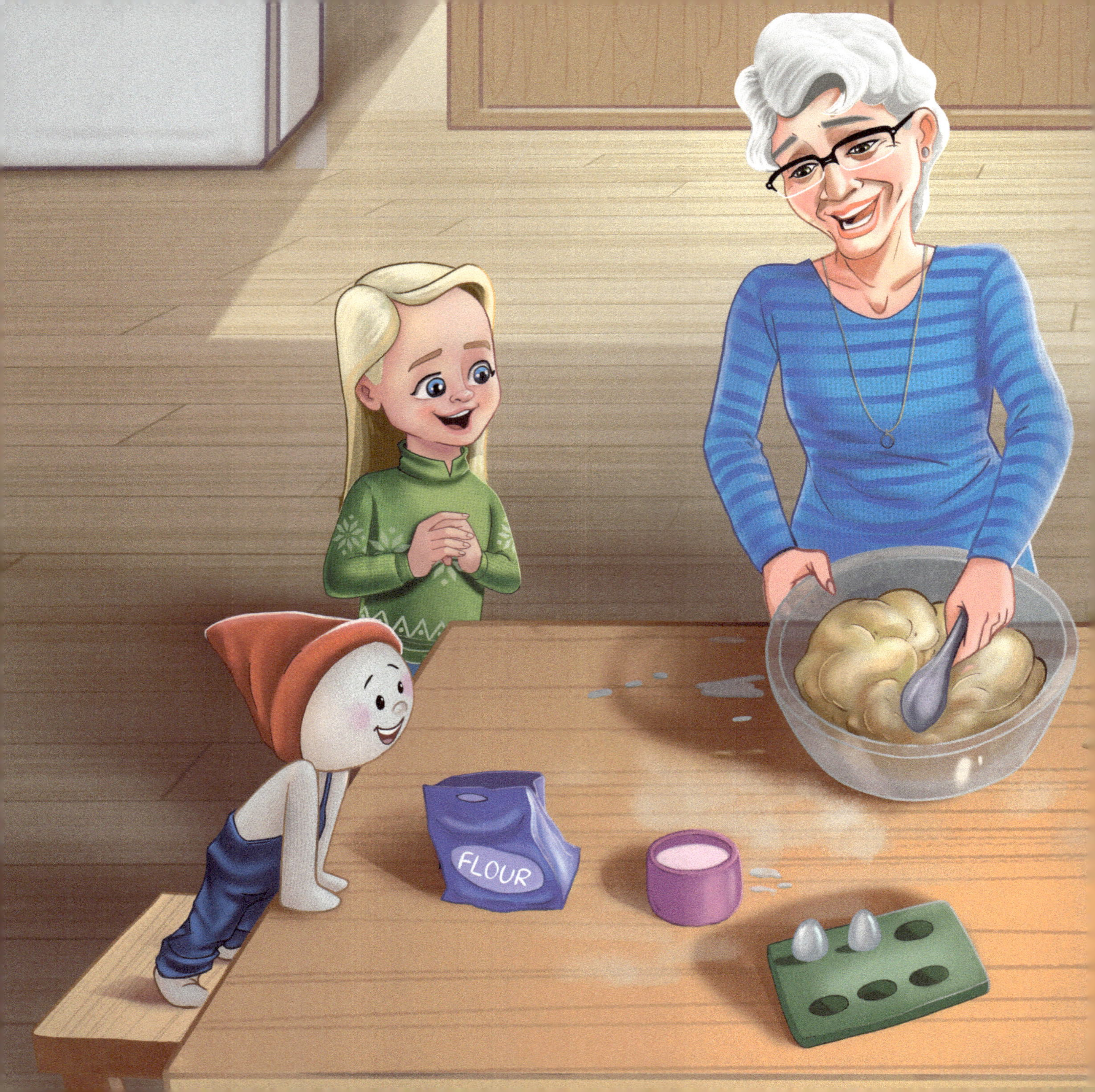
FLOUR

We all help clean it up so we can mix the **dough.** It's a good thing Grandma is helping us!

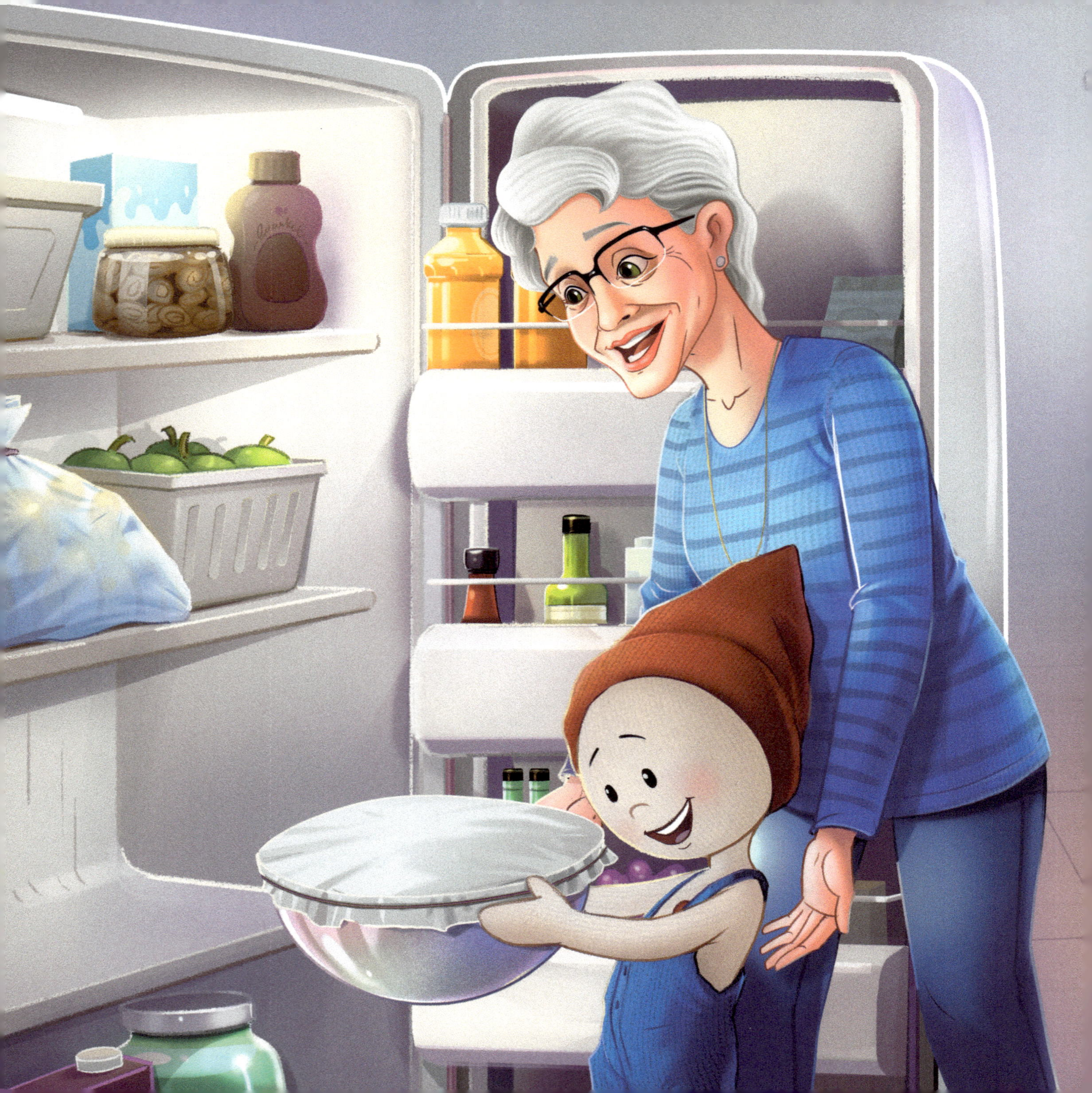

When the dough is ready, we put it in the refrigerator and that's where it will stay all night.

We sure do have a messy **kitchen** to clean up again.

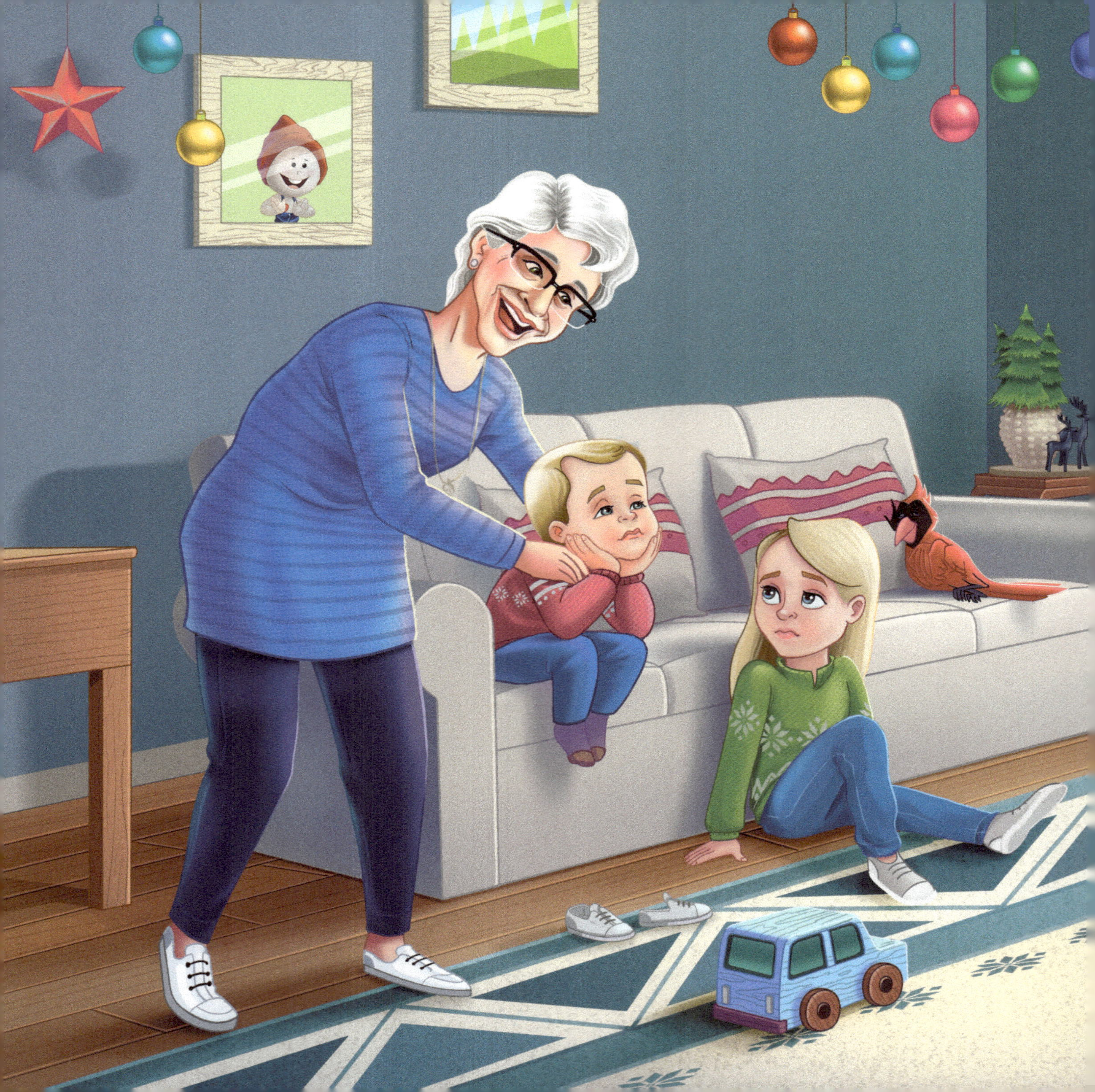

Waiting until **tomorrow** for the Kringla is so hard. Grandma says, "Be patient."

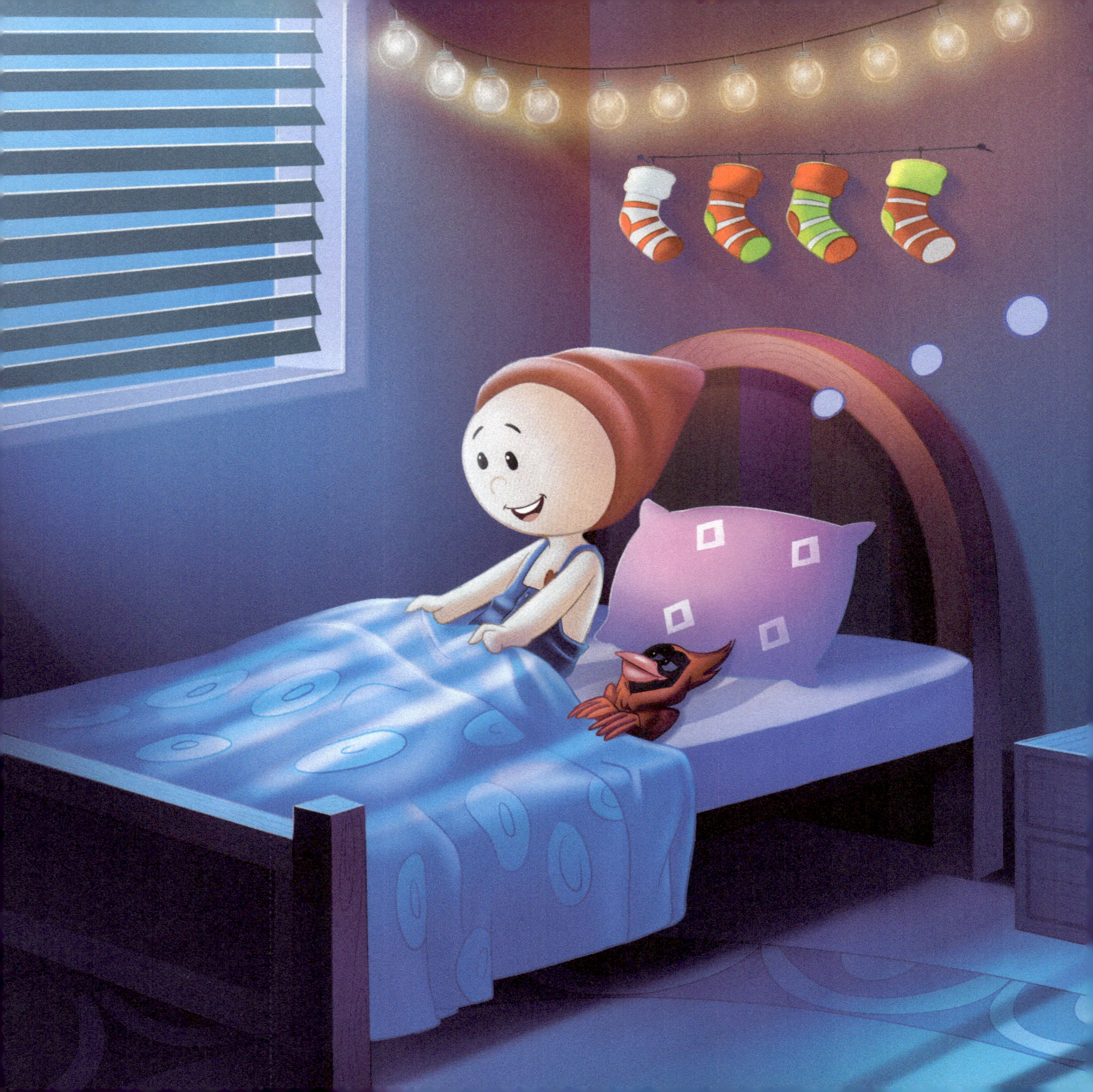

Maybe if I go to bed, tomorrow will get here faster. When I go to sleep, I'll **dream** about cookies—big cookies, small cookies, all kinds of cookies.

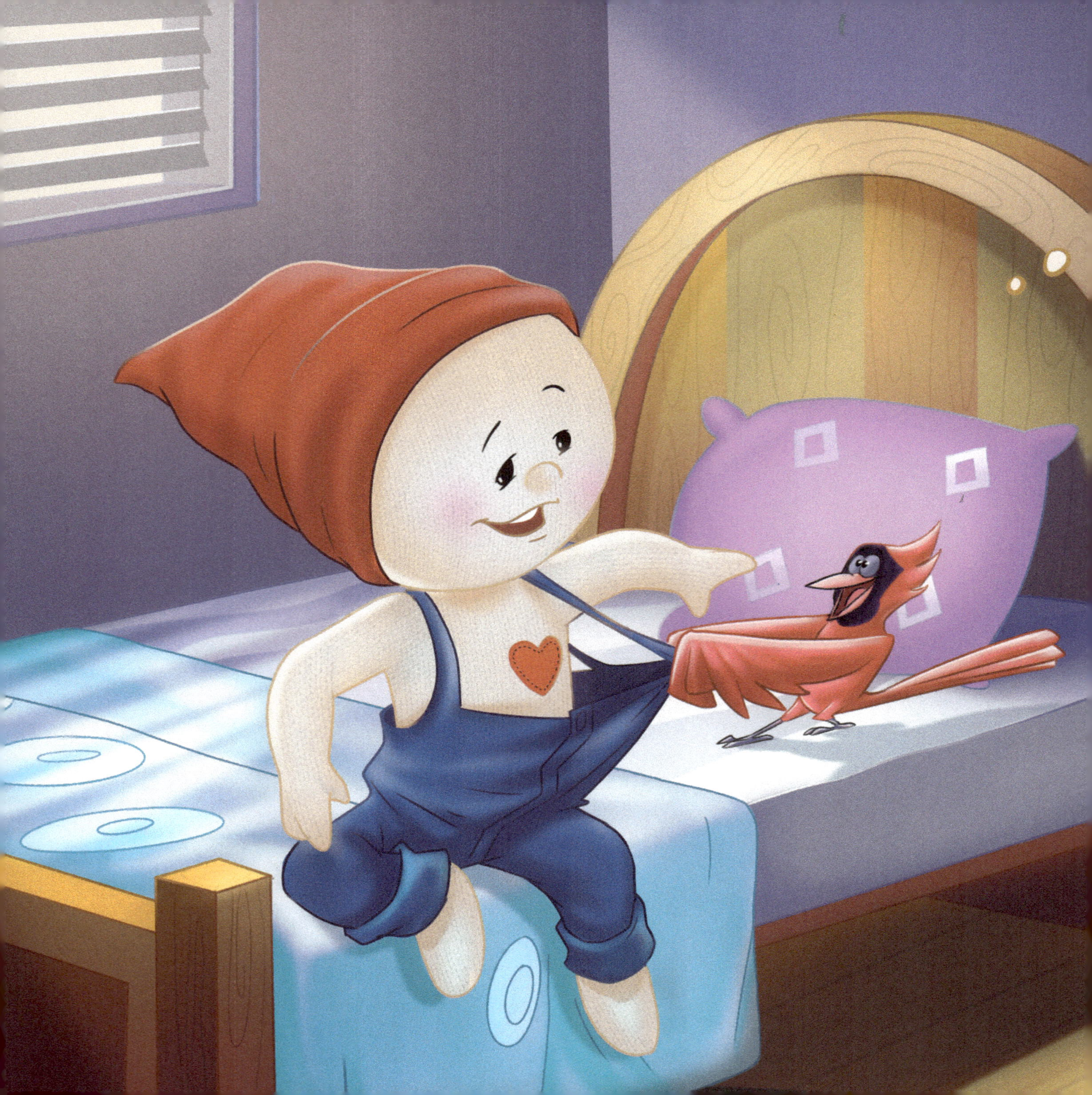

Finally! It's Kringla **baking** day! I think about the Kringla. I wonder... how will I eat mine?

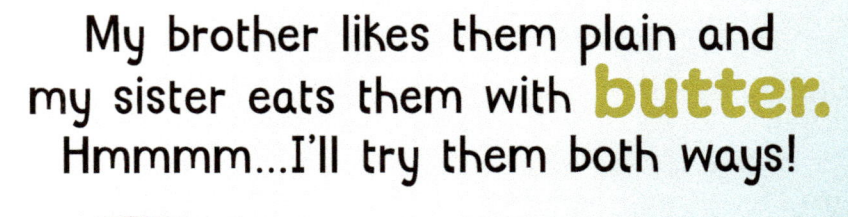

My brother likes them plain and my sister eats them with **butter.** Hmmmm...I'll try them both ways!

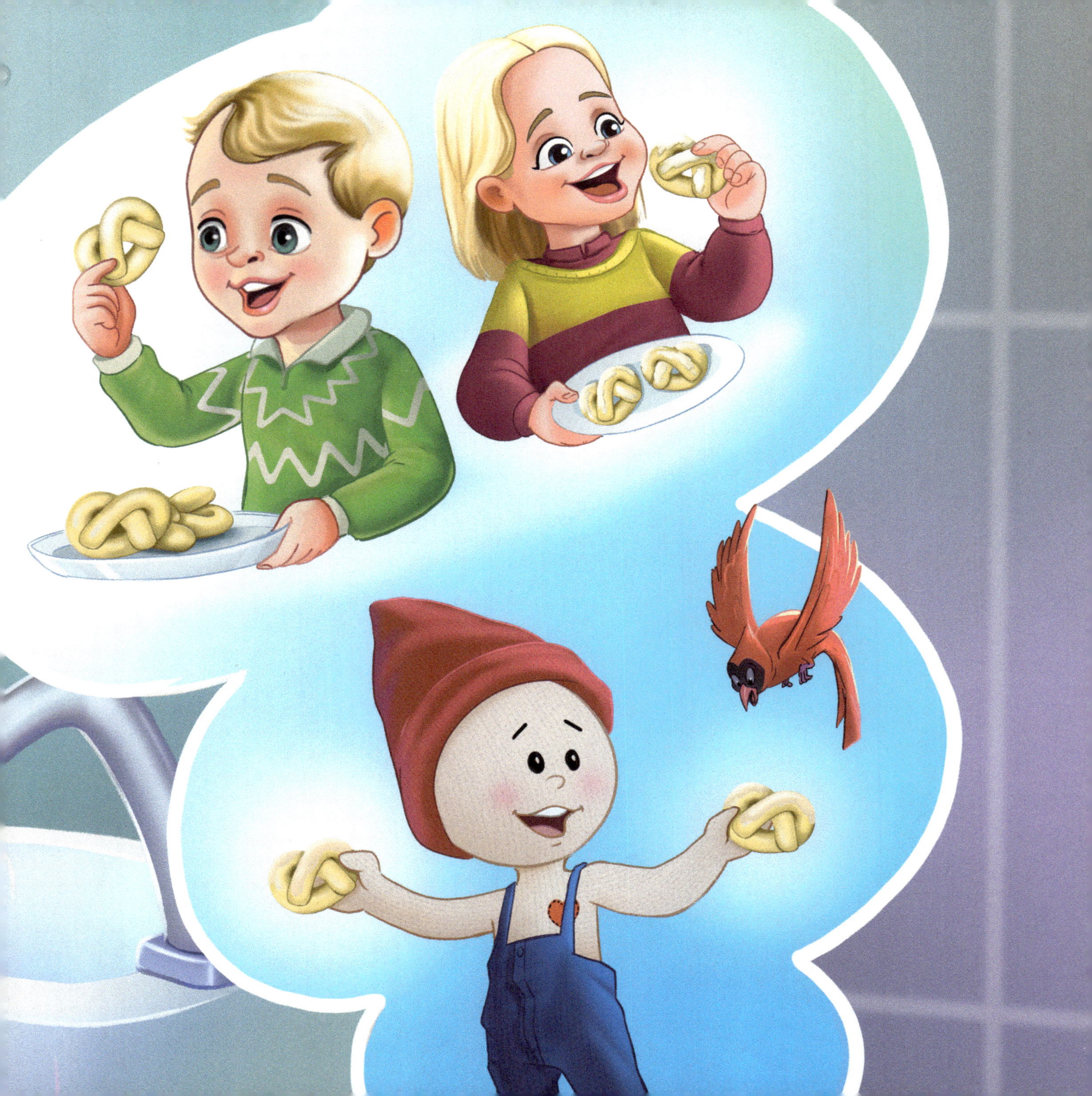

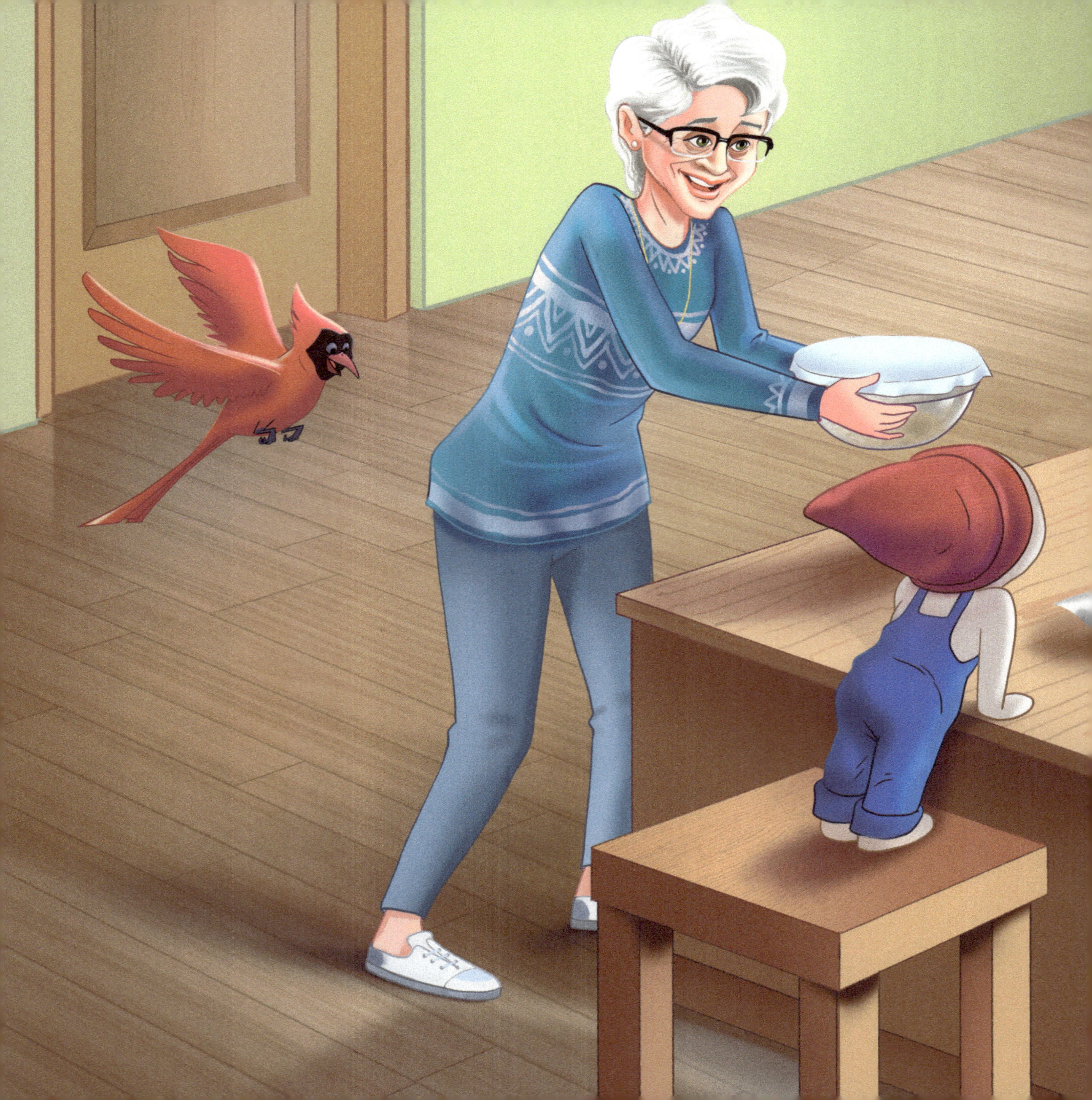

Grandma helps me carry the bowl of dough. It's pretty heavy. We put flour all over the **table.**

We put a **large** spoonful of dough on the flour and start rolling it with our hands. We roll it into long ropes, then cut into pieces that we form into pretzel shapes and place on a baking sheet.

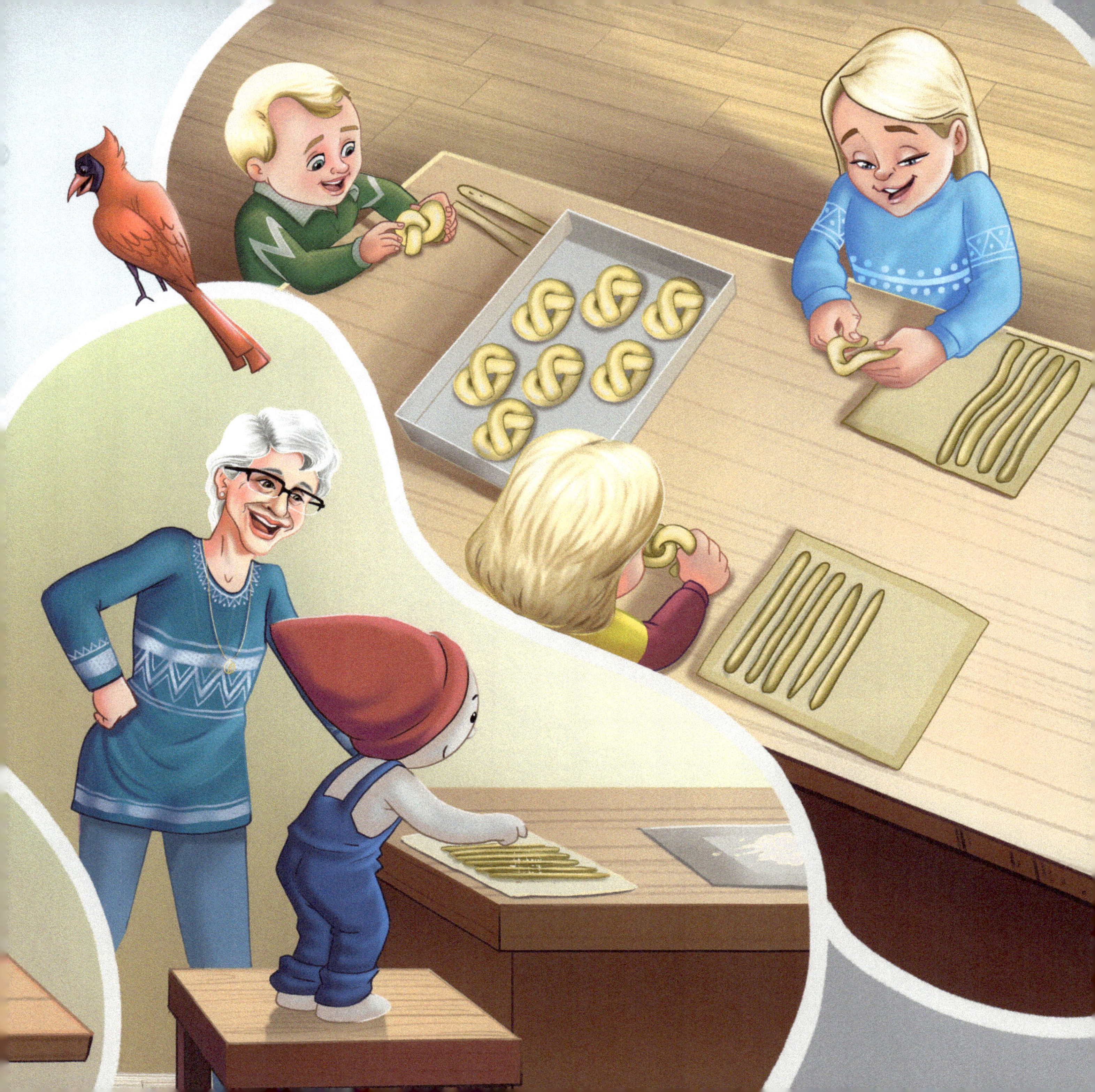

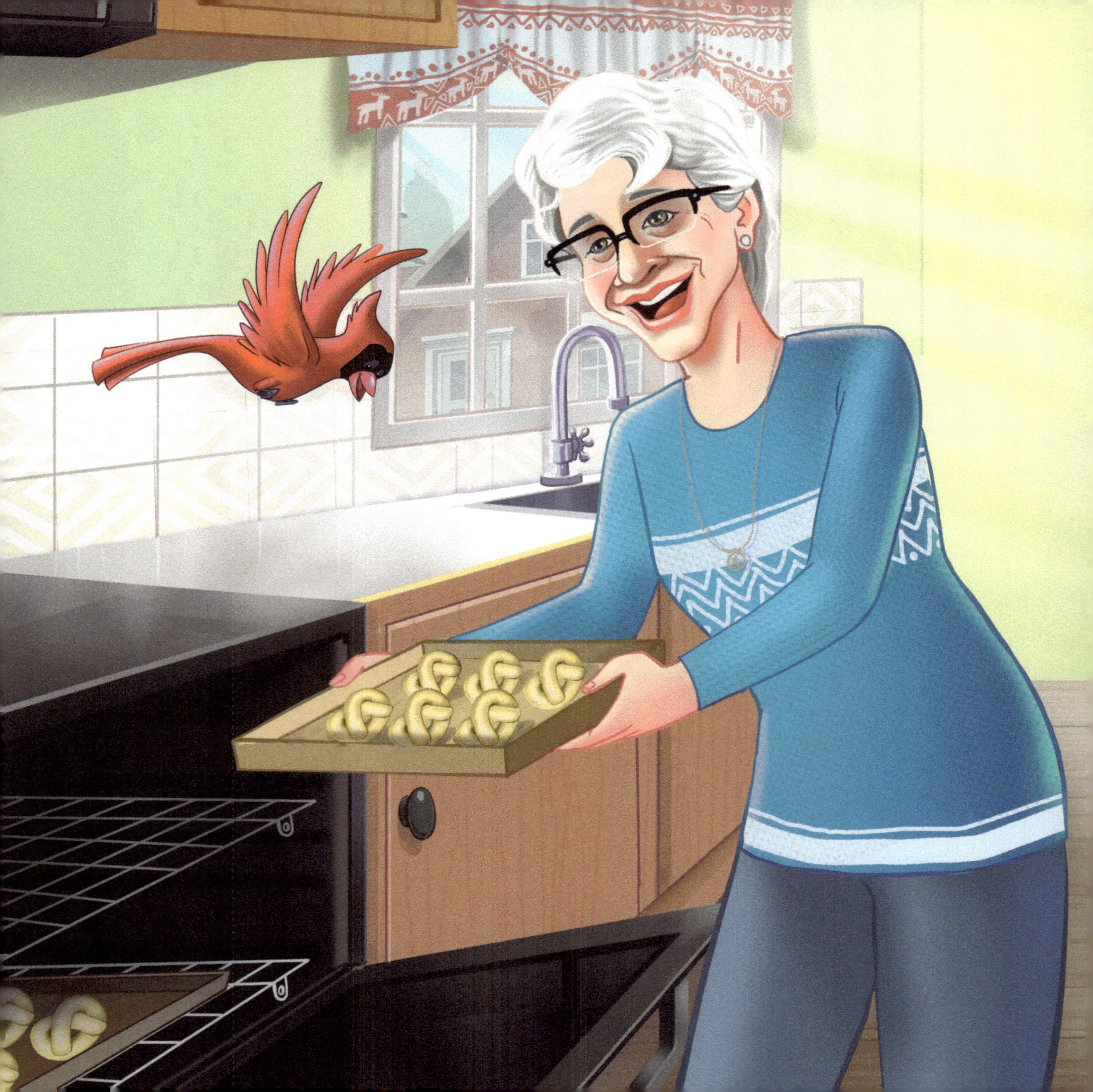

Grandma puts the baking sheet in the **oven** for us. We wait patiently for the Kringla to bake.

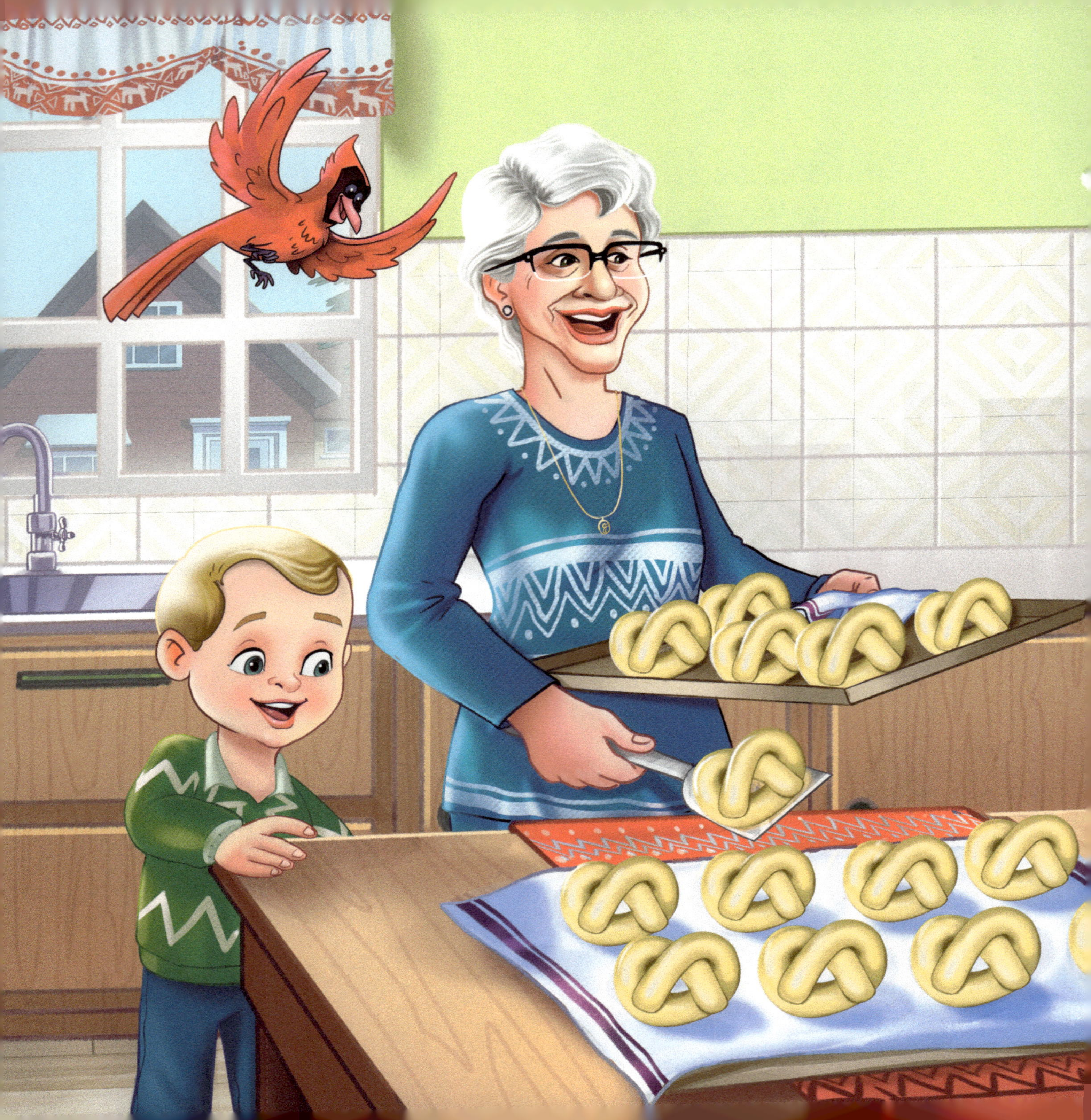

Pretty soon, Grandma takes the Kringla out of the oven. Now we have to **wait** a bit for the Kringla to cool.

I'm going to eat one now because
I like them **warm** from the oven.
Everyone takes a Kringla. They taste amazing!

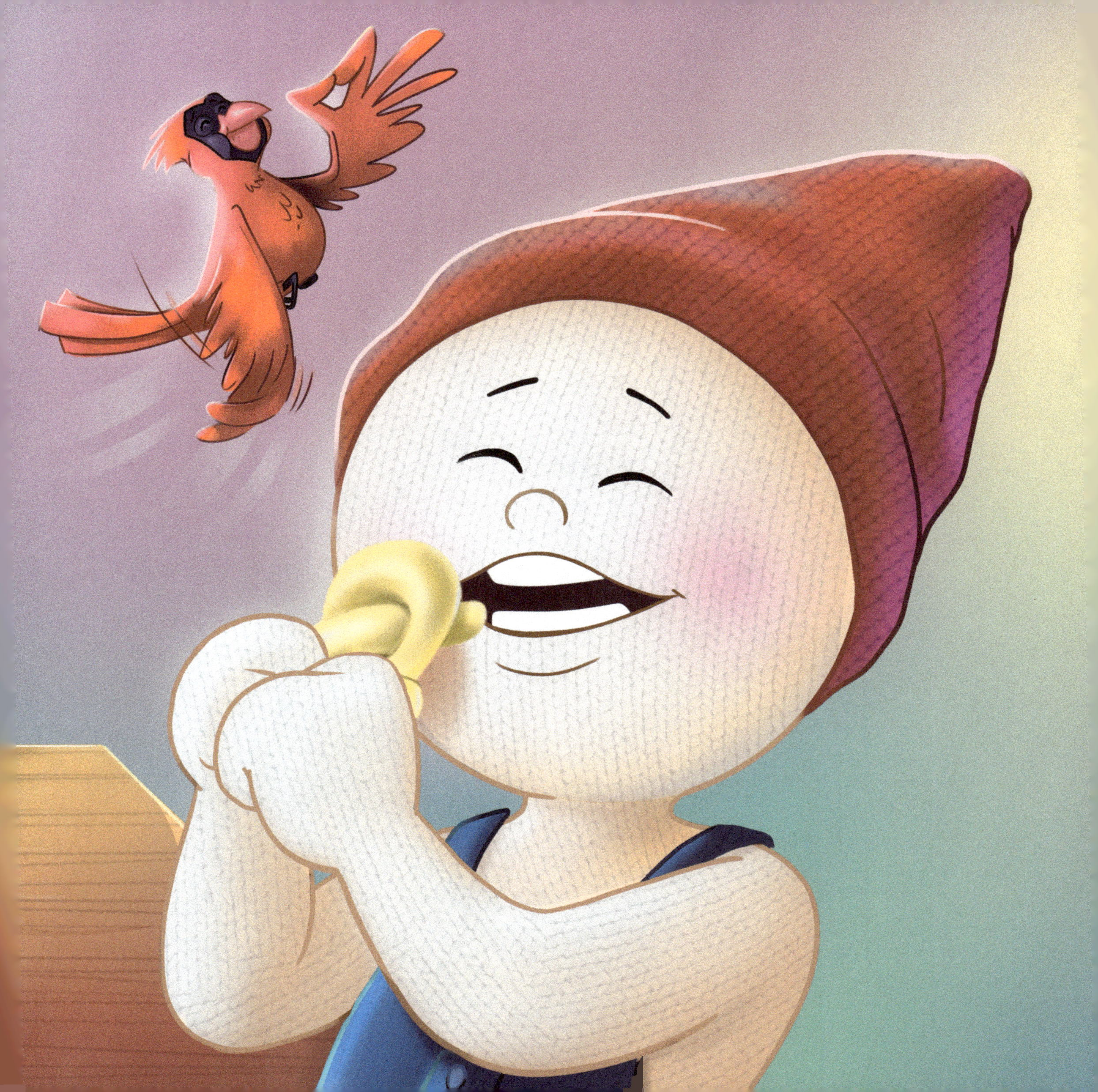

Thank you, Grandma!
Let's do this again tomorrow!
Merry Christmas!

GOD JUL

Kringla Recipe:

- ✓ 1 cup granulated sugar
- ✓ 1/3 cup butter (softened but not melted)
- ✓ 1 egg
- ✓ 1 cup sour cream
- ✓ ½ cup buttermilk
- ✓ ½ teaspoon salt
- ✓ 1 teaspoon vanilla
- ✓ 2 teaspoons baking soda (mix in sour cream)
- ✓ 3 ½ cups all- purpose flour
- ✓ Extra flour to roll out

Mix all ingredients together. Refrigerate overnight. Roll into ropes on a floured board. Form into a pretzel shape as you place on a baking sheet.

Bake at 475 degrees for 5-6 minutes until just barely brown. Makes 3 dozen.

The Story of Seven Cookies

The tradition of baking seven types of cookies during Christmas in Norway, known as "syv slags kaker," is a cherished holiday custom. The cookies can be baked, fried, or made with a special form or iron. It is said that you're not truly Norwegian without seven types of cookies to offer guests.

Some common cookies include:

- Sirupsnipper (syrup diamonds)
- Berlinerkranser (Berlin wreaths)
- Sandkaker (tart-shaped cookies)
- Krumkaker (delicate cone-shaped cookies)
- Smultringer (little donuts)
- Goro (rectangular biscuit made with a decorative iron)
- Fattigmann (dough cut and woven into itself then deep-fried)
- Serinakaker (buttery almond cookies with almonds and pearl sugar)

Though there are eight cookies mentioned above, families often have their favorites. Our family, for example, includes Kringla in the seven and chooses from other family favorites as well. Historically, families baked even more—sometimes up to 11 types—reflecting their wealth. Kringla, especially beloved among Norwegian-Americans, sparks the biggest debate: butter or no butter?

There are words highlighted in multi-colors throughout this story. Those words are shown below in Norwegian, with pronunciation.

Grandma	—	Bestemor (BEH-steh-mor)
Make	—	Lage (LAH-geh)
Recipe	—	Oppskrift (OHPP-skreeft)
Gather	—	Samle (SAHM-leh)
Eggs	—	Egg (EHGG)
Dough	—	Deig (DIE)
Kitchen	—	Kjøkken (SHUHK-ken)
Tomorrow	—	I morgen (ee-MOR-gen)
Dream	—	Drøm (DREM)
Baking	—	Baking (BAH-king)
Butter	—	Smør (SMUR)
Table	—	Bord (BOORD)
Large	—	Stor (STOOR)
Oven	—	Ovn (OHVN)
Wait	—	Vente (VEN-teh)
Warm	—	Varm (VARM)
Merry Christmas	—	God jul (GOO YOOL)

About the Authors

Teresa and Lavonne are sisters who enjoy traveling and spending time with family. Sharing a passion for their Norwegian heritage, they began writing stories that include Norway's language and culture. This story is personal and includes their mom and three of her grandchildren. Teresa and Lavonne also love Christmas and they will eat Kringla any time of the year.

Thank you to Prayan Animation Studios, Bobbie Hinman, Praise Saflor, April Cox, and our families for their advice, ideas and support.

For more information on The Uff Da Sisters,
the Gnome Adventure Series books, the gnome doll,
activities, teaching materials and other
Nordic products, see the following:

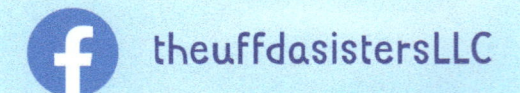

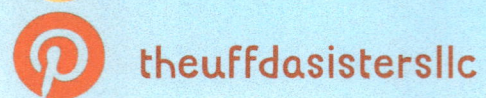

theuffdasistersLLC

theuffdasisters

theuffdasistersllc

THE UFF DA SISTERS

Theuffdasisters.com

Copyright © 2024 Nordic Heart Press
All Rights Reserved. No part of this publication may be produced in whole or in part, or stored in a retrieval system, or transmitted in any form, or by any means, electronic, mechanical, photocopying, recording, or otherwise, without written permission of the author.

Illustrations by Remesh Ram
Book Design by Praise Saflor

Publisher's Cataloging-in-Publication data

Names: Bjelland, Teresa, author. | Bjelland, Lavonne, author. | Ram, Remesh, illustrator. Title: Gnome makes kringla / written by Teresa Bjelland & Lavonne Bjelland; Illustrated by Remesh Ram. Series: The Gnome Adventure Series
Description: Ankeny, IA: Nordic Heart Press, 2024. | Summary: Gnome and their siblings are thrilled to bake kringla with Grandma! Amidst the fun and mess, they learn valuable lessons about teamwork, patience, and family traditions.
Identifiers: LCCN: 2024914788 | ISBN: 978-1-961285-12-5 (paperback) | 978-1-961285-13-2 (hardcover) | 978-1-961285-14-9 (ebook) | 978-1-961285-15-6 (audio)
Subjects: LCSH Christmas--Juvenile fiction. | Baking--Juvenile fiction. | Gnomes--Juvenile fiction. | Norway--Juvenile fiction. | Animals, Mythical--Norway--Juvenile fiction. | Folklore--Norway--Juvenile fiction. | Grandparents--Juvenile fiction. |BISAC JUVENILE FICTION / Holidays & Celebrations / Christmas &Advent | JUVENILE FICTION / Cooking & Food | JUVENILE FICTION / Family /Grandparents | JUVENILE FICTION / Toys, Dolls & Puppets
Classification: LCC PZ7.1 .B54 Gn 2024 | DDC [E]--dc23